Prim

Angus Gaunt

Prime Cuts

Mockingbird
An imprint of
GINNINDERRA PRESS

For Kate, with love

Prime Cuts
ISBN 978 1 74027 459 3
Copyright © text Angus Gaunt 2007
Cover image: Jemima by Pascal

First published in this form 2007 by
GINNINDERRA PRESS
PO Box 6753 Charnwood ACT 2615
www.ginninderrapress.com.au

Contents

A Porky Prime Cut

When Krystel Smith was fourteen she became friendly with the new owners of the Blue Duck Café. Their names were Paul and Gareth Browne and it was the first time they had lived outside the city although they had been coming up to the high country for years.

The café had never done very well under the previous owners. It was a town where coffee was drunk out of cracked mugs at laminex kichen tables, where breakfast was a couple of pieces of quick toast and where a meal out was either a pub steak or the Chinese banquet at the bowling club. There were not many people who considered a three-dollar cappuccino to be money well spent.

It was Paul who spoke to her first. 'Hello,' he said as she stood in the street watching him busy with the paint rollers. He was working bare-chested, his shirt hanging down from the waist of his jeans even though it was not particularly warm. He came to the door. 'What's your name?'

Krystel was too fat to wear jeans and her hair hung in unbrushed strands over her cheeks. Nobody ever asked her name, except at school, so she told him. She was fascinated by the pink hairlessness of his chest, and the way it almost seemed to glow under its light sheen of sweat. Most men, when they took their shirts off to work, were deeply tanned.

Paul explained how they were giving the café a facelift, a new lease of life. The walls would be yellow, the counter and the tables purple. 'I like my colours to be bright,' said Paul. 'Don't you?'

'Yes,' said Krystel, even though she had never really thought about it.

The café and its new owners were the talk of the town for a few days. When they opened for business many people who had never set foot in the previous establishment came in for a look. All were greeted cheerily by Paul and because there was nowhere to hide, many of them sat down and ordered a coffee. It was all very nice, they agreed, but an undertone implied that the new owners were fighting a losing battle before they had even started. They had been comfortable with the old place, which could be safely ignored, its grumpy owners treated with a sort of mild derision. It had been like the pub, hopeless and rundown, but fuel for the satirical way they boasted of their town to themselves, their secret pride and comfort in its insularity.

*

At lunchtime, Krystel and her new friend, Selina Cleary, sat astride the wall at the bottom of the playing fields.

'What about your dad?' said Selina, rolling down the hem of her school dress where she had been displaying a bruise the size and colour of a ripe plum.

'He used to, but he doesn't any more. He still smacks my little sister, though, if he can catch her. She normally runs away.'

'You're lucky.'

Krystel had never thought of herself as lucky before. Now she wondered whether, in fact, she was. 'My mum slapped me in the face last week,' she offered.

'Mums,' said Selina. 'Hardly counts.'

'I reckon my mum is as strong as my dad,' said Krystel. 'She's got a lot of muscle on her. Dad's just got,' she hesitated to say the word, 'fat.'

'Mine's not,' said Selina quietly. She sketched a pattern in the dust on the top of the wall, then swept it away and started another.

Behind them were all the yells, cries and thumps of the school at recess; another wall of sound.

Krystel started to sketch her own pattern. Suddenly she smiled to herself. 'My dad farts all the time,' she said.

'Mine too!' Selina giggled. 'When he thinks no one's around. Yesterday I came into the room when he was watching TV. He was wafting it with his hand. Like this!'

Both girls were giggling now.

'He didn't say a word when he saw me there. He just went red in the face.'

'Mine's the same,' said Krystel. 'What did you do?'

'I got out of there. For two reasons!'

They were rocking backwards and forwards now, almost hurting themselves with laughter.

'My mum's as bad,' said Krystel when she could speak again. 'She claims she doesn't do it but she does.'

'Everyone does!'

Selina clenched the wall with her knees, raised her buttocks and let forth a little crack. Krystel tried to do the same but collapsed in a heap. The laughter came out of her in little sobs. In the back of her mind she saw her mother walking away from her in her wide track pants. Her exhilaration was spiced by the knowledge of this little betrayal.

'Sitting with smelly Smithers now, are we?' It was Heather Packard, walking past with her little entourage.

Selina made a face but did not say anything. She knew if she did she would get into a scrap from which she could not possibly emerge the winner. Krystel did what she always did when she found herself in the vicinity of Heather Packard: she kept her eyes fixed to the ground. To risk meeting Heather's, she knew, was asking for it. The two of them maintained their positions until the danger had passed, which it did soon enough.

Krystel was well aware that Selina had been part of the entourage until recently. She had no idea why she had been pushed out but she was not going to risk anything by asking. She remained silent and waited for Selina to talk.

'Don't take any notice of her,' Selina said. 'She's only tough when she's got her little gang around her.'

'She's a bully,' Krystel ventured.'

A classic bully,' Selina agreed. 'Scratch the surface and she's just a coward.'

Krystel peeled the lid off her lunch box. 'Want to share my Mars bar?'

'Mmm!' Selina nodded eagerly.

*

Krystel's route to and from school took her past the café at least twice a day.

In the mornings Paul was often putting the sign out on the pavement when she came past. 'Good morning Krystel,' he'd say brightly. 'Cheer up, it may never happen!'

Once Krystel replied, 'It already has.'

Paul thought this was hilarious but after that he just stuck to the plain good morning. In the afternoons when it was quiet she would sometimes stop for a chat. The chat normally consisted of Paul asking her questions about school and her family. He was especially interested in her brother, who was sharing a flat in Sydney and worked as a waiter in a restaurant.

One day, as Paul was talking to her, he suddenly said, 'Look at me, Krystel.'

Krystel looked up.

He took her chin between his thumb and finger and said, 'As I suspected. You have got a pretty face hidden away there!'

She could not remember how it happened, but at some point she started going into the café on her way home. This was how she met Gareth. He spent most of his time behind the scenes, cooking, but at this time of day the pressure was off and he was out at the front with his dish cloth folded neatly over his shoulder. Gareth did not chat away as easily as Paul, and there were a few awkward silences between them at first.

Then one day Krystel turned up as they were discussing what to do about the counter.

'The trouble is,' said Paul. 'It looks so stark and forbidding. What it needs is a softer touch, but I'm just not sure how to go about it.'

Krystel looked at the smart new counter with its coat of gleaming purple paint. She hardly understood what he meant, but remembered a time, years ago, when her father had given her mother a bunch of flowers and how much it had brightened the room having them sitting there on the table. 'How about a bunch of flowers?' she suggested.

Paul looked at Gareth, who raised his eyebrows. 'I think the girl might be onto something there,' he said.

'I think she just might,' Gareth agreed.

They spent the next ten minutes discussing the type of flowers that might be appropriate, the shape of the vase and where they should be positioned on the counter.

Krystel did not take much part in this conversation but when they came to the vexed question of the expense of fresh flowers she made another suggestion. 'You could get artificial ones. If you didn't want them to look the same all the time you could change them, same as you'd change real ones,' she said. 'As long as you had enough of them.'

Once again they seemed to be blown away by the idea.

'I love that,' said Paul. 'I really do! We could have a competition to see who can make the best arrangements out of the same materials. Krystel could join in too.'

'She'd probably win every time,' said Gareth.

'Good point. She might show us up. Better not let her anywhere near the flowers.' He went over and put his arm across her shoulders. 'Only joking, darling,' he said. Then he pronounced her their 'principal design consultant'. They wouldn't make any more decisions, he said, without consulting her.

*

Ray Smith skewered his last piece of steak and chased gravy around the edge of the plate before posting it into his mouth.

'Where are they from?' he asked, chewing. His shirt was unbuttoned all the way down, revealing thick blond chest hair above his blue singlet.

'Melbourne,' said Krystel, who had finished hers and now had more than one eye on *Home and Away.*'

'City folk, eh?'

Krystel nodded, almost imperceptibly. She rarely gave a direct answer to a question from her father as she had found that his conversations were mainly with himself.

'City folk,' he muttered again.

In the background, Krystel's mother, Lauren, moved around the kitchen trying to calm the baby which she had perched high up on her shoulder. Her large hands showed they were not unaccustomed to the gentleness required. The baby belonged to Krystel's elder sister, who snoozed in a chair, exhausted from interrupted sleep.

'What are their names?' said Ray, as though the answer to this question might provide fuel for his suspicions.

'Paul and Gareth,' said Krystel quietly.

'What was that?'

'Paul and Gareth,' said Lauren.

'Paul and Gareth,' he repeated to himself. Then, 'They've got the same surname, haven't they?'

'Yes.'

'How does that work? They're not brothers, are they?'

'I don't know.'

'They don't look like brothers. How'd they get the same surname?'

'Perhaps they just happened to have the same surname to start with,' Lauren suggested, smiling to herself and dumping the baby onto his shoulder.

Automatically his hands reached up to pet the child.

'It's not as though they're called Spariopoulos,' said Lauren.

He looked up at his wife, frowned then sighed. 'Get me another beer, Krys.'

Krystel did as she was told. Her father removed the cap by twisting it against the arm that was holding the baby and took a long draught. His pink lips glistened. Meanwhile, Lauren cleared the plates from the table.

'Seem to have plenty of money, don't they?' said Ray.

'Why do you say that?' asked Lauren.

'They must have spent a fair bit doing the place up.'

'I think they've done it up quite nicely.'

'Been in there, have you?'

'Course I haven't. Not to buy anything anyway. I had a quick sticky the day it opened.'

'I don't mind what people do in private, but I don't want it shoved down my throat.'

'Nobody wants that.' Lauren had to agree with her husband, even though she had been inadvertently charmed by Paul when he had made a point of talking to her in the street. So she concentrated her thoughts on Gareth, who had not. 'Certainly not me.'

'You won't catch me setting foot in that place, with them,' he went on.

'You never set foot in the place when the Clearys owned it.'

'I never spent any money there. You can get perfectly good coffee out of a jar at home for free. I used to have a chat with Bill Cleary once in a while, miserable old bastard that he was. Never spent a cent with him though. Can't see the point in cafes.'

'Some people like them, just like some people like pubs. Especially when they're passing through and they want somewhere to break the journey for an hour or so.'

'Who passes through here?'

'Paul said there was a bit of tourist trade,' said Krystel. 'They were hoping to build it up.'

'Well, I hope for their sake there is,' said her father. 'Because I can tell you I'm not the only person in this town thinks the way I do. You want to be careful with them, Krystel, specially when you're there on your own.'

*

As she got to know them better, Krystel found herself liking Gareth even more than she liked Paul. Paul was the extrovert, the charmer, the one who always had something to say and never shied away from saying it. With Paul you saw what you were going to get straight away. Gareth revealed himself slowly. He was the cook, the behind-the-scenes man. Unlike Paul, he never spoke without thinking and what he did say tended to go straight to the point.

What she especially liked was listening to the banter between them. It hinted at a whole new world. Already they had nicknames for some of their regular customers. Old Mrs Dale, who hobbled in every morning at ten for her 'cupaccino', they christened 'the walrus'. Nervous Mary Thwaites they named, with much giggling, 'gerbil', and to Mr Copeland, the self-important local councillor, they gave the rank of colonel.

They displayed open disdain for what they saw as the unsophisticated culinary tastes of the town.

'He asked for a medium-rare steak,' said Paul. 'So Gareth cooked him a medium-rare steak in the traditional manner. When I served it to him he called me over, like this.' He curled his index finger. 'I thought he must have found a slug in his lettuce or something but he just made a little cut in the middle of his steak and said, "Look at that. Blood." It was pink, as it should be. I took it back to Gareth. "Burn this one to a cinder, darling!" I said. God help us if anyone asks for well done. We'd have to burn the whole place down!'

Krystel particularly liked the way they involved her in their elaborate little artifices. She did her best to play her part and giggled along with them even though she could not always have said what it was they were laughing at. She found herself quietly thrilled when they talked about people behind their backs. The notion of betrayal stirred something visceral in her.

The menu itself caused endless discussion. It was written on a chalkboard above the counter which could be removed and carried over to a customer who was too short-sighted to read it. It was written up and decorated by Gareth, who had nice handwriting and who was constantly fiddling with it. At one point he wiped it clean and wrote in large letters, 'COFFEE $3'.

'It's the only thing we ever sell,' he insisted. 'So why not cut to the chase?'

Sometimes, to trick Paul, he would add non-existent items. Paul would be taken by surprise by a customer peering at the chalkboard and enquiring after a 'cheese-bucket steak' or a 'frotho marinato'. It became part of the joke that he would answer, 'I'm sorry, we're all out of that.'

Once Gareth added something called 'Porky prime cut', which caused Paul to explode with laughter when he saw it.

'What am I going to do when someone asks for that?' he said.

'Tell him it's his lucky day,' Gareth answered mysteriously.

*

Lunchtime at school, and Selina was still in the locker room, zipping and unzipping the compartments on her backpack. Everybody else was outside now.

Krystel was waiting at the door. 'Are you coming?' she asked.

'Yes,' said Selina, shortly. 'In a minute. You go ahead.'

Somehow she had agreed to have her lunch on the wall with Krystel again. At the time she had been on the outer with Heather and her gang, but just that morning Heather had said hello to her as though nothing had happened. Now the very air around Krystel Smith seemed undesirable

'What are you looking for?' Krystel said.

All Selina seemed to be doing was zipping and unzipping the zips. 'Nothing!'

Krystel turned to go. 'I've got another Mars bar today,' she said.

Selina waited until she was safely out of range. 'Stuff your face with it then, you fat pig!' She muttered.

*

'Have you got a boyfriend, Krys?' Paul asked her one day as Gareth was teaching her to make scones.

Krystel shook her head.

'There must be someone you like,' he persisted. 'Maybe in secret?' Paul liked conversations of this sort and never allowed them to be strangled at birth.

Krystel wanted to concentrate on kneading the flour, using the tips of her fingers as Gareth was showing her. It was surprisingly hard work. 'No, not really.' Images of Justin Timberlake flitted through her mind.

'Not really!' Paul pounced. 'Sounds like a definite maybe to me. What do you think, Gar? What's she hiding from us?'

Gareth grinned but said nothing. It seemed he was on Krystel's side.

Paul started to ask her about school in general. 'What do you get up to with your mates?' he said. 'All sorts of mischief, I bet!' He started talking about a particular teacher he'd had and a day when they had got their own back on him.

Krystel concentrated on rubbing the butter through the flour. She had never known what it was like to do something with a group of mates, except for isolated incidents when she had been swept up in something that was going on and the others had been too caught up in their excitement to notice they had an impostor in their midst; either that or it had given them a temporary generosity of spirit. When everything had calmed down again, she never found herself any closer to being part of anything.

'Who's your best friend?' Paul was saying. 'Girls always have a best friend, far more than boys.'

'Selina Cleary,' she muttered with quiet anxiety. Even the mention of her name, she felt, was to invite Selina's scorn. Only that morning Selina had been part of a group, led by Heather Packard, who had collectively held their noses as they rushed past her.

'Selina Cleary,' Paul repeated. 'Nice name.'

'Is she any relation to the old bloke we bought the café from?' asked Gareth.

'Oh yes,' said Paul. 'She must be his granddaughter at least, eh?'

Krystel shrugged. She knew what was coming next.

'Can't be too many Clearys in a town like this.'

As he whittered on it occurred to her that he was the sort of person who would be certain to somehow get the message back to Selina and she would be humiliated all over again.

Please don't say anything, she wanted to say. Instead she said, 'Do you know Mr Cleary?'

'Of course we do!' said Paul. 'Gareth and I spent many a happy evening with him learning the ropes before we signed on the dotted line.' He winked at Gareth.

'One happy evening,' Gareth corrected him.

'Maybe it was just the one. I do tend to exaggerate sometimes, Krystel, as you've probably noticed. It may not have been all that happy either, come to think of it. We've got to go up and see him about something later this week. Can't wait!'

'Are you going to ask him about Selina?' Krystel said, so quietly she wondered whether she would have to repeat herself.

'I expect so,' said Paul, but Gareth interrupted him.

'He won't,' he said firmly. 'I promise you he won't.' He smiled down at her, a great calming presence.

Krystel breathed easy. She wondered whether she should take another Mars bar tomorrow, or maybe Selina would prefer a bar of Cadburys Dairy Milk.

*

'I'm not condoning it,' said Ray Smith. 'But I'm not surprised it happened. People just don't like that kind of thing round here.'

That morning Gareth and Paul had woken to find eggs smashed against their front door and several terse, unambiguous messages printed on the walls, in black permanent marker. They had had to hide it temporarily by sticking up sheets of butchers paper because it had proved impossible to scrub away.

'As long as they keep it to themselves,' said Lauren, perfectly attuned to what he was talking about.

'But they don't, do they? They don't keep it to themselves. You can't even walk down the street without having it shoved in your face. They've even got the place painted bloody purple!'

'It's mainly yellow actually. They've just used purple for the trimmings. I think it's quite nice.'

Ray shook his head in exasperation. She just didn't get it, or she wouldn't, or as he sometimes suspected, she did and she was laughing at him.

'I wonder who it was anyway,' said Lauren.

'Kids,' said Ray. He used a tone of voice which implied that adults might have made a better job of it.

'Well, I hope they don't feel unwelcome here,' continued Lauren.

'What do you mean?'

'I hope they don't think whoever did it represents the community as a whole.'

Ray grunted. He could not guarantee that this was the case. Only the day before he had been discussing it in the pub next door. Every once in a while, his thoughts had strayed to what might be going on just two walls away, and he had felt the hairs uncurl on his chest.

'Apart from anything else, it's been so good for Krystel,' said Lauren

'What do you mean?'

'They're teaching her to cook. She told me she wants to be a chef. It's the first time I've ever known her to be interested in anything.'

'Well, I'd prefer if she didn't go there.'

'Why ever not? I'm all for it.'

'I don't trust them with her, that's all.'

Lauren resisted stating the obvious, that their daughter was more likely to be safe with Paul and Gareth than with any other pair of men. But she knew his real fear ran elsewhere, that he was more afraid of an insidious contamination of their lives with the wantonly exotic.

*

The next morning, Paul was on his knees with a dustpan and brush, carefully sweeping up the last little traces of glass from the hole in the window where someone had thrown a rock through the night before. 'Eggs are one thing,' he said. 'Eggs you can clean off. I don't even mind a bit of graffiti, God knows I've had plenty of that in my time. But this is material damage. This is the sort of thing that could put us out of business.'

Cracks radiated in all directions from the hole like a cartoon depiction of solar rays. It was the first time Krystel had seen Paul lose his sunny disposition.

Krystel, who had been walking past on her way to school,

surveyed the outer edges of the wooden floor for stray shards. She discovered three large ones, which prompted Paul to declare that there was nothing for it but a complete re-vacuuming.

'Wonder what the legal position is,' said Gareth, 'if someone cuts themselves on the result of an act of vandalism?'

'I think I'd rather avoid finding that out.'

'I know,' said Gareth. 'I was just wondering.'

'I'm wondering too,' said Paul. 'I'm wondering who would want to do this. Who would want to do a thing like this, Krystel?'

Krystel had a very good idea who, if some of the comments she had heard at school were anything to go by. The same people had been responsible for various other acts around town; letter box explosions, chooks being strangled and the like. But those acts were more or less anonymous, they were not directed at anyone in particular. This time there were clear targets, as evidenced by the graffiti. Paul looked as though he might be about to burst into tears, so Krystel excused herself, saying she didn't want to be late for school.

'Yes, go on, darling. You run along. We don't want you getting into trouble too.'

She now had a regular job there, for pay, on Saturday mornings. The pay was minimal, almost derisory, but even so it was more than they could afford. It had been Gareth's idea to formalise the arrangement. He felt it might be a way of getting them onside with the town, those elements of it that resented their presence as outsiders. It was also a sort of insurance for a time, far in the future, when they might be able to leave the café open while they went away for the weekend.

*

Sitting astride the wall at the bottom of the oval, Krystel peeled the wrapper from her lunchtime Mars bar. She broke off a chunk and lowered it into her mouth, taking care to direct the tapering toffee interior between her lips. She liked the cooler weather because the chocolate stayed firm and could be broken like this. Also, it did not melt against the fingers the moment it was touched. She chewed softly.

'Hold your noses, everyone!' It was Heather Packard and her gang, marching past with their faces in the air. They put their fingers up to their noses with almost military precision. After a few seconds, the fingers came down from one.

Selina Cleary broke ranks and came to perch on the wall in front of Krystel. She raised her paws like a meerkat and begged. 'Pwease,' she said in a little meerkat voice. 'Pwease-pwease-pweeeease!' She had scrunched up her eyes and sucked in her cheeks.

Krystel laughed.

'Don't take any notice of them,' Selina said, with a nod towards Heather and gang, who were now wheeling around in curiosity.

Krystel preferred to take notice of them. She was actually flattered that they had not simply ignored her as they went by.

Wordlessly, she opened her lunch box. Inside were gleaming stacks of chocolate; Mars Bars, Dairy Milk, Cherry Ripe, the lot.

Selina's eyes widened. 'Where'd you get these?' she said.

'Bought them,' said Krystel simply. 'At Woolies.' This was how she had spent her first Saturday's earnings from the café.

Selina took several seconds to sort through the different bars, before finally selecting a Picnic.

'Good on yer, Krys,' said Selina. 'Good on yer.'

By now the rest of them had formed a circle, close enough to see the contents of the lunch box.

The question was asked again. 'Where'd you get them?'

'She bought them,' said Selina. 'At Woolies.'

Krystel rather wished she had not told Selina the truth. She would have preferred them to think she had nicked them. The girls stood around, all eyes on the contents of the lunch box.

Eventually it occurred to Heather Packard that she ought to take control, or at least assert herself. 'Can I take one?' she said.

'OK,' said Krystel, as though the thought had only just crossed her mind. If she had been a different kind of person she might have observed that this was the first time Heather had said a civil word to her.

Heather reached across and took out the first item that came to hand – no undignified demurrage time for her. Krystel did not offer the box around for the others but waited for them to ask, each in turn, so that she might have occasion to confirm or deny the request. They reciprocated by not thanking her.

Then, as the group wandered away, Selina broke off and came back down to the wall. She was holding Heather's Mars bar. 'Can she have a Cherry Ripe instead?' she said.

Without a word Krystel exchanged the bars.

'Hey,' said Selina. 'There's a party tomorrow night at her place. You can come if you want.'

This was such unexpected news that Krystel had trouble processing the information. She looked blankly at Selina.

'Heather said it was OK.'

'Are you sure?'

'Course. Everyone's going.'

*

After five minutes with Paul and Gareth, Krystel rather wished she had not mentioned the party.

'Parties,' said Paul. 'Remember them, Gar?'

'Is that,' said Gareth, 'where you get together with your friends and spend all night imbibing foreign substances into your body?'

'You do remember! It's so long since I've been to one I'd almost forgotten what they were all about. Maybe you can take us with you, Krys. We wouldn't be any trouble, honestly.'

Krystel hardly knew what to say. She had the distinct impression that Paul was serious, that if she had said yes he would have jumped at the chance to tag along. Fortunately she did not have the opportunity to say anything before he was off again.

'If we can't go to a party, maybe we should bring the party to us. Maybe we should throw one of our own. What do you think, guys?'

'We could invite all our new friends,' said Gareth.

'Yes. Now let me see, who would we have? Krystel of course – actually it would be her party too. You could bring some of your friends, Krys, and your family of course, and your brother too, if he's down from Sydney. We could invite the gerbil, the walrus…'

'I'm beginning to see a theme,' said Gareth.

'Actually,' said Paul. 'We shouldn't be so mean about them. Mrs Dale was very good to us this morning, after the smashed window incident. Did you hear about that, Krys? She made her entire family come in and buy our all day breakfast. And when I say her entire family…'

'There must have been at least twenty of them,' said Gareth. 'I ran out of bacon twice.'

'And in several cases their heads did not even grow beneath their shoulders. Actually some of them were perfectly sweet, weren't they, Gar? I take back every bitchy remark I've ever made about my friend Mrs Dale, all except the one about her being as tight as the proverbial. She even managed to get away from this one without spending a cent, didn't she, Gar?'

'Oh yes. She quietly put her coffee on her nephew's bill.'

'But that's all right. She can keep having her pensioner's discount as long as we last here, as far as I'm concerned.'

*

Krystel sat on the corner of her bed, last Christmas's cosmetics set open beside her. On the other bed her younger sister, Kylie, sat watching her carefully. Their father had placed a tall wardrobe in between the beds to give the impression of two separate rooms, but it just looked cramped. Krystel started with eyeliner. She had a vague idea that make-up could be used to tease out the pretty face which Paul had alluded to. She applied a couple of lines, blinked into the mirror and turned to her sister.

'You look like a cat,' said Kylie.

Krystel raised her eyebrows. A cat was not necessarily bad.

'A cat wearing a wig.'

Krystel wiped her face clean with a tissue. In the space between the bed and the wall her mother's iron quietly seethed on a towel. They had spent the previous hour using it to straighten her hair. Kylie, who had some experience of this even though she was only ten, had taken the lead, controlling the iron and manipulating the position of her sister's head on the towel. The result was not quite as Krystel had envisaged, but the smell of singed hair certainly testified to Kylie's industriousness. Krystel took the brightest of the lipsticks out of the box.

'Whose party is it anyway?' asked Kylie.

'Just some mates.'

'I didn't know you had any mates.'

'Course I've got mates. Just cause I don't bring them home all the time.'

'You've never even had a sleepover.'

'I have.' Krystel felt herself colouring.

'Who with?'

Krystel remembered times far in the past, nights arranged by her mother, with little girls who were daughters of her mother's friends. 'I've had sleepovers,' she said. She turned round and puckered her lips at her sister.

'Now you look like a bird – no, a fish. A fish with a wig.'

Krystel turned back to the mirror and rubbed away the lipstick with a tissue. Kylie was right, she looked better without it.

'Paul reckons I'm pretty,' said Krystel.

'Paul at the café?'

'He says I have a pretty face.'

'What would he know?'

'What do you mean? Do you think I have? Honestly, I mean.'

Kylie considered. 'It's all right,' she said.

Krystel decided to make do with this as a compliment.

'Cheryl said they were arguing about you when she was in there with her mum.'

'What were they saying?'

'One of them didn't want you serving the customers. They said you put people off.'

'Which one was that?' asked Krystel.

'I don't know. I didn't ask.'

'Was it the one that does the cooking or the one that serves?'

'I said I don't know!'

Krystel suddenly felt as though a clean hole had been cut in the fog of her complacency. She imagined each of them saying it in turn. In both cases the result was pain and betrayal, a feeling she wanted to physically reject.

She leaned forward and picked something up off the table. 'See that? That's the key, the key to the café.'

'Did you nick it?'

Krystel had half a mind to say yes. 'They gave it to me.'

'Why?'

''Cause.'

'What are you going to do with it?'

'I don't know. I could get in there any time I want. Even in the middle of the night. If I wanted.'

'Are you going to?'

Krystel remembered what Paul had said when he dropped the key into her hand. It was a sign of their trust in her, a mark of faith. 'I could,' was what she had intended to say, until she observed the way her little sister was staring at her, eyes agog. She smiled mysteriously and said, 'I might.'

*

Krystel's father drove her to the house on the other side of town where the party was. 'Maybe I should come in with you,' he said half-heartedly, trying to remember what his wife would have done in the circumstances. 'Say g'day to the parents, make sure there's no grog…'

'Don't worry, Dad,' said Krystel. 'Her parents are really strict. They don't even drink themselves.'

Ray Smith looked up, instantly relieved. 'Oh well, that's all right then.'

Krystel leaned over and kissed him on the cheek, then shuffled back across the seat and opened her door.

'Half past ten, remember? I want you standing out here,' he jabbed his forefinger down into the earth. 'At half past ten on the dot.'

'OK, Dad.'

He drove away and Krystel was left on the dark verge. From the front of the house there was little evidence of anyone at home, let alone a party. But the door was open, so she walked straight in. The first room she passed seemed to be dark and unoccupied, but she could hear something going on at the back. In the kitchen three girls from her school were mixing drinks, one of them giggling more loudly than seemed warranted. They were dressed in dark clothes, with well-pierced ears and black-lined eyes. Krystel hardly recognised them at first. She immediately wished she had made more of her own eyes.

One of them squinted in her direction. 'Who asked her?' she said in an undertone, and the three of them leaned in towards each other, giggling.

Krystel went through into the backyard, where it now seemed there was a lot of noise. There was a standard patch of lawn with a few shrubs around the outside and a hoist in the middle, fanning out like some giant skeletal flower. The whole area was lit by a single light bulb above the back door. Through an open window metal music boomed.

There was also a strong fiery smell, the source of which was soon evident: fireworks. Boys were rushing down the yard, disposable lighters in their hands, setting the fuses then retreating with loud conspiratorial sniggers. Every now and then there was a shower of sparks and the sharp smell of gunpowder as something went off. At one point a lighted rocket fell over and pointed in the vague direction of the house causing yelling and screaming and ducking for cover, all underlaid by almost hysterical giggling. Someone scampered down and jabbed at it with his foot, managing to steer it in a more acceptable direction before it shot out across the grass.

Krystel was looking around for faces she knew. It was hard in the light and with the way everyone had dressed and made themselves up, but she found she recognised most of them from school if she stared long enough. All the girls, she noticed, were holding cigarettes like slim extra digits. At one point some of the figures perched on the outdoor furniture glanced in her direction. She thought she saw Selina's face. She walked around for a better view but they did not turn again. Eventually she took up a position next to the door of an old outhouse and observed the proceedings from there. Krystel was well used to being an observer. She did not mind that no one talked to her. The fact of being present at the party was enough.

The girls who had been mixing drinks in the kitchen brought them out on trays and placed them on the outside table, shooing away the ones who had been sitting on it. They poured them out from tall jugs into glasses, mugs and paper cups where they were soon swept up by greedy hands. When they had finished, Krystel ventured forward and poured the residue from one of the jugs into the last of the coffee mugs. She saw that the girl she'd thought was Selina really was her. Their eyes locked for a second and Selina gave a bare nod before turning back to her breathless conversation. Krystel hovered for a while, wondering whether she had been invited to join the circle. It was dominated, as usual, by Heather Packard. She was telling stories about her boyfriend, Mitch Craig. Krystel stood there, sipping from her coffee mug. Underneath the bland lemonade there was the taste of something fiery and illicit. Eventually someone asked her whether she was going to stand there all night and she returned to her doorway. She was well aware that she took up more space than other people.

Soon the last of the fireworks was finished and the boys came and perched with the girls. Mitch Craig plonked himself in Heather's lap. She squealed and squirmed and they swapped places. Everyone watched as they kissed for the best part of a minute, then Mitch pulled away, apparently sated. The talk resumed while Mitch, with

Heather on his lap, flicked his lighter on and off with his free hand. Its tiny flame seemed to be out of proportion to the effort he expended in producing it. He kept glancing around as though looking for something else to set on fire.

Over the next hour and a half, Krystel went to the toilet seven times. This way she moved about sufficiently often for any observer to assume she was properly engaged with the ebb and flow of the party. She always resumed her position by the outhouse but because she was moving around so much and because she spent longer each time locked behind the toilet door she was able to pretend that she was taking up the position out of choice.

When she came back for the last time, the tone of the gathering had changed. The metal music had been replaced by something more soulful and there was a single conversation going on amongst the group on the outside furniture. They made a little tableau under the weak light, with people sitting on the chairs, on the table and perched on the window ledge. The ones in the centre were doing all the talking. Everyone else just listened. Krystel was able to insinuate herself into the outer reaches of the circle without being noticed. She leaned against the kitchen wall and watched and listened too.

They were discussing the smashed window at the café. At first Mitch denied any involvement but as he sensed the mood turn to approval he started to imply that he had actually been lying.

Eventually he started to boast. 'That was just a taster,' he said. 'If I got serious they wouldn't know what hit them.'

'When are you going to get serious, Mitch?'

'I said if, not when. I don't know, it depends whether I can be bothered.'

'They're all right,' said one of the girls. 'We normally go there for breakfast on Saturdays. The one that serves is quite funny.'

'I wouldn't set foot in that place. It's disgusting what they get up to.'

'But they don't do it in the café.'

'How do you know? They might. They might be doing it right now!'

'On the counter!'

'Yuk!'

An expression of disgust made its way around the group. Krystel mouthed her own, curling her lips then grinning like the others to show that she was not afraid to contemplate the subject further. A couple of the boys carried on the speculation, raising the stakes higher and higher until the laughter turned to howls of outrage.

'People like that,' Mitch declared. 'Should not be allowed to exist.'

'So what are you going to do about them?' asked one of his lieutenants, who derived a vicarious thrill from the outlandish ideas Mitch seemed prepared to put into practice.

'I've got something in mind for them,' Mitch said mysteriously.

'What?' Heather asked, wide-eyed on his lap.

'You'll see.'

'I'd be careful if I was you. They're paranoid about security after the window and the graffiti.'

'How do you know that?'

'I told you, we go there for breakfast. My mum sometimes goes there for coffee too. They talk to her.'

'I wonder when they'll get the message that they're not wanted around here?'

'Hey,' someone said. 'Doesn't smelly Smithers work there?'

Several heads turned as one in Krystel's direction. Her heart jumped. She had been quite unaware that her presence had been noticed.

'You work in the café don't you, Krystel?' Selina repeated.

Krystel nodded.

'What's it like working for a pair of…'

Mitch Craig interrupted. 'Hey, Krystel,' he said. 'Would you mind terribly being put out of a job?'

Krystel nodded, shook, then nodded her head again. She had never been addressed by Mitch Craig before. She had been unaware that he even knew her name.

'Well?'

All eyes were now on her. She felt suddenly dazzled, as though a spotlight had been thrown on her. But she straightened her back and moved towards the table. She could feel the key in her pocket, pressing against her groin. Everyone was silent as they waited to see what she would do.

'What'll you do without all that free food to stuff your face with?'

Krystel hardly heard what was being said. She thrust two fingers into her pocket. A few seconds later the key was out, gleaming under the gaze of Heather and Mitch and the others.

*

'Gar, are you awake?'

'I am now.'

'Did you hear something?'

'Only you.'

'No seriously. Listen for a minute.'

'…'

'Well?'

'No, can't hear anything.'

'I'm sure I heard something. It sounded like the front door.'

'Go down and have a look then.'

'You come with me.'

'No, I'm tired.'

'I don't want to go down there on my own. There might be someone there.'

'Don't then.'

'But what if there is someone there?'

'For God's sake, Paul, just go back to sleep.'

'I just thought I heard something, that's all.'

*

'Lucky,' said Ray Smith, 'it wasn't burnt to the ground.'

'They said it might as well have been,' said Lauren. 'There was that much damage done. When I went past, it was black all the way up the outside.'

'I wonder who it was?' asked Ray.

'Who said it was anyone?'

'Course it was someone. It wouldn't have set fire to itself.'

'It could have been an accident, an electrical fault or something.'

'After all the other stuff that's happened?'

Lauren had no answer, however much she would have preferred to think that sort of thing did not happen in their town. 'If it was deliberately lit,' she said at last. 'How did they get in? None of the windows were broken or anything.'

'Maybe they forgot to lock up last night.'

'No, they always locked up. They were extremely careful about that.'

'Why? This isn't bloody Melbourne. People don't need to lock up at night round here.'

This was so self-evidently incorrect that Lauren had half a mind not to respond. 'After all the other stuff that's happened?' she said. 'I think they'd be justified locking the place.'

'Perhaps it was an inside job,' Ray suggested.

'What do you mean?'

'Perhaps it was them. Maybe they realised they weren't wanted round here so they did it for the insurance.'

'That's mad!'

'It happens.'

'But they'd never get away with it. And why would they risk their own lives like that? Their bedroom is directly over the café.'

'God, don't make me think of that!'

'Well, they're quite lucky to be alive, you know. If the smoke gets you in your sleep you might never know anything about it.'

'But if they'd done it themselves they wouldn't have been asleep.'

'That's just such rubbish, Ray, and you know it. They'd never do something so stupid.'

'Old Charlie Dale tried that, remember? He thought if he was actually injured in the fire he wouldn't be a suspect.'

'Old Charlie! He didn't think that one out very well.'

'He didn't think anything out very well.'

'He didn't think at all!'

They both chuckled as they remembered the silly old bugger.

'Anyway,' said Ray, 'I'm not condoning what was done. But people like that don't belong round here. They'll be much better off back in Melbourne.'

'They might not want to go back.'

'Are you kidding? Course they will. They'd be crazy to stay here after what's happened.'

'Well, I'd be sorry if they went. I liked them, in spite of everything. And they were so kind to Krystel. She'd really been coming out of herself lately, don't you think?'

Ray Smith grunted. He thought of the girl he'd dropped off at the party the previous night, almost unrecognisable with her hair and make-up. 'Yes,' he said. 'She had.'

The Kick

Barbara has an itch, but she doesn't want to scratch. Even if she did she wouldn't be able to, so it's just as well. The itch is in a place she cannot reach with her fingers. It's like a moth behind her stomach wall, fluttering. Once upon a time it would have driven her to distraction but now it simply makes her smile. It's a reminder of something she wants to remember.

They'll be organising that place for her now at what's-is-name village. They've been waiting for this, this proof she can't look after herself, and they surely have that now. They are, of course, only thinking of her. It'll be easy enough to move her out. Most of the work has already been done. The only furniture left is what was hers in the first place, that and a few other items that have been deemed the bare minimum to sustain her until she leaves.

This is Barbara, a stranger in her own house, only it's not really her own. She stands around like a ghost while members of her sister's family inspect what is on offer. It's stifling hot inside with all the people and the clutter. They've opened the windows but it makes little difference because there is hardly any breeze outside. Hopefully there will be a southerly along later.

Barbara is looking forward to getting rid of some of the clutter. When they moved in, Jean brought all the furniture from the property, which had space to spare. Although she gave a lot of it away, there is still far too much for a house this size. Everything is now marked with red or white sticky labels. Red means it can be taken away today, and there is a van waiting outside for the purpose. White means it is available but stays in the house until Barbara leaves. And then there are the things that will go with her, labelless, principally her armchair and the TV. These, withered fruit of her eighty-one years, were hers in the first place.

Some of these people she only knows from photographs. They all seem to know her. They greet her by name. There is even the occasional peck on the cheek. Overseeing the day are her sister's sons, Andrew and Neil, her nephews, and to her the word still connotes small boys in shorts. The labels were Neil's idea. He watches with quiet satisfaction as everybody moves through the house, like visitors to an auction showroom. Neil is the younger of the two and has battled all his life to make his mark against his smarter, quieter, inscrutable older brother. Now their mother (Barbara's sister) is gone and her worldly goods are being distributed. The grandchildren are starting to set up homes of their own. Nice old items of furniture will take pride of place among brick and plank bookshelves and self-assembly computer desks.

She makes her nephews nervous, she knows this. They just don't quite know how to take her, so mostly they avoid talking to her and when they don't they speak slowly and clearly as though she is deaf, or gormless, or a child. She has always been their aunt but she has only appeared fleetingly and in some circles is always referred to as 'poor Barbara'.

Now Neil is explaining to her the thinking behind the labels. Under the terms of the will, he stresses, she is allowed to stay in the house as long as she is capable of looking after herself. Even as he says these words she feels she is being scrutinised for signs that it is not so. Andrew has even given her the name of a doctor he knows in the area. Anything, he says, anything at all, just mention his name. Yes, she thinks, mention his name and he'll reach straight for the drawer where he keeps the certificates: 'In my professional opinion, Miss Barbara Leach is no longer…'

The place is worth well over a million for land value alone. With one of his town-house developments Andrew reckons he could double it. Jean and her husband bought the place back in the early sixties for a holiday home, the fruit of a couple of decent seasons. When they retired they surprised everybody by selling the property and moving in here permanently. Then, when he died she surprised everyone again by asking her unstable sister to move in with her. An act of charity it might have seemed, but Barbara feels they both gained something from the arrangement. For herself, these years have been the happiest of her life. She has never felt more stable. And now, all too suddenly, they are over.

So, Neil is saying, we thought you'd need the table, and just a couple of the chairs and things. We can't have you eating off the floor, can we? And Barbara pretends not to hear his little joke just to spare herself the trouble of laughing. She knows they would be more than happy to see her eating off the floor. With that kind of behaviour they would need no further excuse to put her into what's-is-name village.

Andrew took them to see it last year, when Jean was still well. He had some interest in the place, she can't remember what exactly. But she can remember Jean's first remark on seeing the institutional dining area. 'Shoot me if I ever get like that.' They giggled the rest of the way around, at the tiny 'apartments' with their tasteful chrome handrails and the restful plants in the lobby ('When someone dies,' said Jean, 'they just pick off a few leaves and hey presto, another wreath!'), at the idea of the nurses rushing from one emergency to the next as the inmates pressed their buzzers at night. Every new feature Andrew pointed out seemed to be another cause for mirth.

He took it in good heart. He was able to trump his mother with the simple observation that the place was making a fortune.

It is as though the family are in a different dimension from Barbara as they move about the house. Each of them has at least one other person with whom they can swap intimate remarks. Barbara starts to feel a sense of disconnection, as though she has been cut adrift from her anchor. A not unfamiliar feeling. She would like to sit down but can't, not yet. The chairs, even the one that belongs to her, are not available to be sat on right now. Then suddenly she is taken by the elbow and steered into the kitchen.

'Come on, Barb, let's go and make some tea.' It's Maria, eight months pregnant, the wife or partner (she's not sure which) of Andrew's eldest. Maria is very young, barely out of her teens. Her skin is smooth and creamy, almost perfect. She asks Barbara where she keeps the cups and Barbara points to one of the two cupboards that she knows. This was Jean's territory, almost exclusively. When she fell ill they relied on takeaway chicken and since her death Barbara has eaten mostly toast.

Maria bustles around the kitchen opening and closing cupboards, peering into the backs of shelves. It is very hot. She digs out a teapot and various extra mugs. Watching her do this gives Barbara a feeling of the narrowness of her own horizons and great swaths of experience she has missed. Jean, it occurs to her, would have been a great-grandmother if she had held on a few more weeks.

Maria chats to Barbara as though they are resuming a conversation that was broken off earlier. In fact they have only met once before this. She is engagingly disrespectful towards her family, her father-in-law, even her husband. The feeding frenzy, she calls what is going on in the other room.

Her husband has his eye on the leather Chesterfield sofa. As the eldest grandchild he believes it should have been his, that first choice of the loot is his birthright. But Neil has other ideas. He has devised a system whereby they draw names out of a hat to determine the order of choice. Neil wants nothing to do with systems that favour the first born. Barbara was born first in her family but she cannot recall a single incident where it told to her advantage. All she can recall is Jean's gradual assumption of the role of elder sibling as she embarked on her own lifelong struggle to cope.

There's a fresh breeze along the cliff-top walk. Perhaps the southerly is on its way. Maria and Barbara progress slowly, taking frequent rests on the benches that mark the route. Here they come, leaning on each other for support. Maria has the straight-backed, splay-footed walk of the heavily pregnant. Barbara has rickety knees. There's an operation she could have done but she doesn't see the point at her age.

Way below them the sea is a deep clean blue. It undulates like a living thing, pregnant in itself. Jean used to say it felt like coming home when she moved down here, and it had been Barbara's idea that her ashes should be scattered from this cliff edge. But Andrew and Neil have recently taken her out to the property where they grew up. They had to get permission from the new owners, who were understandably reluctant to have a complete stranger fertilising their lawn for evermore, but were happy for her to be scattered anywhere else as long as they were not told where it was. It's what she would have wanted, they said, and who was Barbara to disagree?

Maria is excited about her baby. A child is all she has ever wanted. 'How about yourself, Barb,' she says, stroking her huge belly. 'Did you ever want a child?'

Well, Barbara thinks, nobody has ever asked her that question before. Not to say she's never thought about it, but in her day a husband was generally considered a prerequisite for thoughts of that kind, let alone the act, so even that dull tweak she felt all those years ago when she was allowed to hold the infant Andrew was accompanied by a guilty pang. She says something neutral in response. She has never really been in a position to think about it. Neutral but true. Nowadays women in her position have other options available to them. It's as easy as going to the supermarket, or so it would appear. She wonders if she would have been tempted. Was that the right word, tempted? Yes, she thought it was.

Sometimes, in the mirror, she catches sight of her own belly as she steps out of the shower. Among the veins and wrinkles it is firm and convex, shaped like the lid of a small saucepan. Never used but yellowed with age, it puts her in mind of a birdless egg.

Suddenly Maria gives a little gasp. She holds her belly.

'What is it?' Barbara asks, concerned.

But Maria's face is warm and flushed and she is smiling. 'The little bugger's kicking me,' she says. 'Here.' She takes Barbara's fingers and places them against her.

At first all Barbara can feel is the warmth of Maria's skin, warmth that gradually resolves itself into the subtle rhythm of blood flow, heartbeat perhaps. She thinks this kicking must be something equally as subtle, something that is only available for a mother to feel, deep down in her mysterious womb. Then it is as if something – yes, a miniature foot, why not? – is pushing out from the inside with all its strength. She feels the imprint against her fingertips. It is quite incredible. She looks at Maria. When she looks away again some seconds later, she is surprised to feel her face still set in a rictus of delight.

Back at the house the feeding frenzy is over. Selected items of furniture are being loaded onto a van from which they are to be distributed among various homes. Maria's husband has his Chesterfield after all. He is thrilled. He greets Maria with a kiss and a cuddle. Maria gives Barbara a wink but Barbara feels happy for him. She is happy that he should get so much pleasure out of owning the sofa on which his grandmother, her sister, spent most of those last few days before she finally took to her bed. She is pleased, too, at how the day has gone for Andrew and Neil.

Her nephews stride about, oiling the family gears with benign patriarchal suggestions. They are happy that there have been no fights, hardly even a raised voice, but their airs of ultimate authority leave no doubt that they could have dealt with them if they had occurred. Barbara makes for the kitchen. She will offer them tea again, she thinks, and this time she will make it herself.

Late in the afternoon, Barbara rises from her chair. The house is empty once again, the southerly has come through and the air is cool and clean. There are large new areas of bare space and the light streams through the big windows onto the polished floorboards. It is as though it has been wiped clean ready for the next phase of its existence.

As she walks across the room, her knee appears to lock. The pain shoots all the way up her thigh, and stays. Barbara gasps. Then she moans. She should not have been so eager to help Maria down those steps. But given the same situation, she knows she'd do it again. She'd take the weight. Maria has promised to bring the baby to visit her after it is born. She would say that of course, and Barbara is accustomed to sudden plan changes but she believes Maria will be true to her word. She wonders where that visit will take place, here or in what's-is-name village.

She has the doctor's number; it's on Andrew's business card next to the phone, just over by the window. He was adamant about writing it out. You don't mess about with your health, he said, and this guy is good. At the village, of course, there are medical staff on call all the time. You don't even have to dial a number. There are special green buzzers all over the place.

At the village she would have her own cosy rooms, one for sitting, one for sleeping, even a little bathroom. There is a big dining room where she would be able to take all her meals, and various other places where she can meet with the other villagers.

Barbara grits her teeth and tries to transfer her weight. It's no good. If the furniture was still here she could use it to sidle around the room. The phone is only two steps away. Perhaps if she allows herself to fall she will be able to crawl across to it. At the village the buzzers are specially positioned for people who have falls. You only have to press one and nurses will come running. Barbara need never be alone again. It will be like living with a family. She considers for a minute, then lets herself fall.

Sons of Silence

The prodigal son arrived at three o'clock. They had seen the dust of his wheels on the plain, one of a handful of wind eddies that seemed to be distributed permanently across it and which moved slowly in one direction or another as the traveller beneath it progressed. This one appeared much like any of the others at first, but gradually distinguished itself by its motion towards them. For several minutes they followed its progress until out of the cloud emerged a horse, a buggy, their son.

'We weren't expecting you until tomorrow,' insisted Elizabeth Russell while her husband caught a loose rein and introduced himself to the horse.

'And I wasn't expecting to be here until tomorrow,' said the prodigal, alighting from the buggy and planting a dusty kiss against his mother's cheek. 'I took the train as far as Newcastle on Thursday, then spent yesterday riding over the range. I'd expected some delays while I made arrangements to come through to Drumwhindle but my timing was perfect for the mail coach and they happened to have a seat spare…'

He had grown his beard, which concealed his shallow chin. It contained a hint of orange underneath the dust. He wore a necktie with a bright-red pattern and boots of soft leather that had only ever seen the dirt of a city street. His name was Roderick, he was the younger of their two sons and it was the first time they had seen him in four and a half years.

Alexander Russell walked around the side of the buggy to shake his hand. Elizabeth quietly viewed the beard, the boots, the clothes. She was looking for a sign of the boy she had nurtured, the perpetually bronzed and dirty skin, the unrepressed energy, the twinkle in the eyes. For a moment she thought she might have spotted the latter, but it was probably a glint from the sun.

'How are things in the big smoke?' asked Alexander.

'Couldn't be better, Father. It's getting bigger all the time, bigger and smokier.'

'Wonderful. That's the spirit!' Alexander Russell had a sudden urge to clap his arms around his son and hug him, to formally invoke the presence of the evidently superior being he saw before him. He deftly transformed this feeling into a hearty slap across the back. 'Doesn't he look fine,' he said to his wife, his red face reddening behind its white whiskers. 'Doesn't he look just fine?'

'Oh, yes,' she replied. 'He looks very fine.'

'A bit narrow across the shoulders but fine nonetheless.' Alexander Russell took the opportunity to measure the width of his son's back with his arm. To his surprise and gratification Roderick did not flinch.

'I've not done an hour's physical work since I've been away,' Roderick laughed.

For Alexander Russell such a claim would normally have been grounds for disapproval. In fact, it was his favourite complaint about city folk, that they were soft and flabby through lack of physical work. He surprised himself for a second time by laughing with his son. 'But doing very well for yourself, I hear!'

'Oh, Father, you would not believe the opportunities there are to make money. Every day another fortune is made.'

'And how many have been yours?'

Instead of answering, Roderick lifted his chin so that the whole of his neck scarf was revealed. He pointed. It was held in place by a gold pin. 'How much do you think I paid for that?' he said, looking from one to the other of his parents and back again.

'I could not say,' said his mother.

'Twenty pounds,' suggested his father gamely.

Roderick shook his head. He mentioned a sum which was more than a labourer would earn in a year, more than the farm currently had in the bank. It brought silence upon both his parents. He was forced to turn his attention to his bags as a way of regaining the energy that the mention of money had seemed to dispel.

That night there were four of them for dinner. They were joined by Tom, Roderick's elder brother, who rode over from the little house on the other side of the property where he lived with his young family. His wife sent her apologies. The younger child was recovering from an unspecified illness and was not considered fit to go out. Unlike his parents, Tom had neither the space nor the means to keep a servant, so there was nobody they could call on to look after the children.

Alexander Russell breathed a private sigh of relief. 'I'll bet you don't get beef like this in the big smoke,' he said.

Roderick swallowed the piece of gristle he had been chewing. His first instinct was to say that they could get anything in the city. But then he remembered something he had promised himself. 'I can't remember when I last had beef like this,' he said instead.

Alexander Russell grunted with satisfaction and posted another slice into his mouth. His mutton-chop whiskers exaggerated the motion of his chewing.

'I'm sure Roderick eats with much more variety than we do,' Elizabeth said.

'I expect he goes to restaurants all the time,' said Tom, whose only experience of one was a couple of trips to Newcastle.

'Tell us about the restaurants,' said Elizabeth.

'Actually I've become quite partial to Chinese food recently,' said Roderick.

'I've always wondered what that was like,' said Tom. 'We don't get too much of it up here. Are there a lot Chinamen there?'

'Hordes. But they invent some wonderful dishes, if you've the taste for that sort of thing.' He strung together some pithy Chinese monosyllables.

They all laughed.

'And what does that mean?'

'I have no idea, but it tastes pretty good!'

'Tom,' said his father 'Have you seen Roderick's tiepin? Show him, Roderick.'

With a moment's reluctance the two brothers leaned across the corner of the table towards each other. It was hard to see in the oil light but Tom discerned something glistening in the folds of the cravat at Roderick's throat.

'How much do you think that cost?' came the inevitable question.

But the answer meant little to Tom. It was more money than he would ever see working on the farm, more than he could ever conceive of spending.

It was Roderick who changed the subject. 'How are the plans for the town, Father? I had a look around on the way through. It didn't appear much changed.'

Alexander Russell was engaged in negotiations with other graziers over the future layout of their township. One side argued that it should be allowed to grow and evolve of its own accord, that nature would see everything right. Alexander Russell was leading the push to impose some order while the chance was still there. He had a grid and a plan to move the main street to some higher ground away from the river which it was now known was prone to flooding. He recounted some highlights from the most recent meeting during which he had got the better of a young upstart who had argued for the other side.

'Melbourne is planned around a grid,' said Roderick. 'And a man cannot get lost. Stand on any street corner and it is the same. North, east, south, west.' He turned a knife on the table for illustration.

'A man can't get lost in our little town,' said Tom. 'Then again, he can't find anywhere to hide either.'

'Some of us,' said his father, 'are looking to the future.'

'It is very important to be forward looking,' said Roderick. 'There's no looking to the past.'

His mother had barely suppressed a laugh at Tom's remark. She looked at the groomed young man with the gold tiepin and looked again for traces of the lovely headstrong boy who had walked out on them all those years ago. He had refused to accept that his fate was tied to this patch of land that his father and uncle had spent twenty years carving out of virgin bush.

Of her two boys he had always been the brighter and more adventurous, although he also had a streak of cruelty that it pained her to notice. Unlike her husband she had not protested too much when he announced his intention to leave. He was born for something better and she was glad to see him released to his ambitions, as she had had to suppress her own.

He had always been his father's favourite but he had been cut off, written out of the will and in the heat of the moment, banned from returning. They were acts Alexander Russell had performed out of a sense of duty to his species, tradition almost.

When a letter finally arrived, two years after his departure, a palpable gloom was lifted from the house. Then, after another similar interval, he announced his intention to visit and the original version of the will was quietly restored.

But this was no longer the original version of her son. He too had suffered from his absence and with his successes she suspected the cruel streak had risen to the fore. He was no longer headstrong as he had been. His every utterance was measured with an eye to its effect.

They were talking about water now. There had been no dispute among the graziers on the need to dam their little river but the project had presented formidable difficulties.

'We almost ran dry in Melbourne last year,' Roderick told them. 'The original dam simply wasn't good enough. The only answer is to start again.'

'Is it?' asked Tom.

'That is what they will have to do.'

'There is nowhere we could start again,' said Tom.

'What about up beyond Cowell's place?' Roderick suggested.

'Then we'd miss out on the Adair stream.'

'But it's a promising idea,' said his father, and mused out loud over its possibilities.

It was not, Tom wanted to say. Apart from anything else it would almost put them at the mercy of that scoundrel Cowell. But his father counted Cowell as a friend. He was blind to the possibility of him being a scoundrel. 'What have you heard about these bores?' he asked instead.

'I've heard the water can be salty, undrinkable,' said Tom.

'But it's just rainwater isn't it?' asked his father.

'It was originally, I suppose. I don't know about the quality of the water, but it is allowing them to open up huge areas for grazing, land that had previously been thought of as good for nothing at all. I know a chap who's decided to put some money into it. He's quietly confident.'

'I wonder whether a bore would be suitable for us here.'

'If it worked it could solve your water problem once and for all.'

'But it would be very expensive wouldn't it?'

'It would be an investment.'

The kerosene lamp in the middle of the table gave off a vaguely unpleasant smell.

'Have you seen much of this new electric light?' asked Alexander Russell. 'A chap I know came back from Tamworth the other day. Said it turned night into day all along the main street.'

'Most of our street lamps are electric now. He's absolutely right. My house will be connected before the year is out,' said Roderick.

'Imagine that!' said his mother. 'Imagine sitting here at night having dinner and the room lit up as though it was daytime. And no smell at all.'

'I've heard electric light is only part of the story. Apparently there are all kinds of possible applications for electricity. There are devices just waiting to be invented; baking ovens, shears, they say electricity could be used to power the trains one day.'

'I don't understand the point of that,' said Alexander Russell.

'No smell, to start with. And there would be no need for them to carry tons of coal behind them,' replied Roderick.

'Is it expensive?' asked Tom.

'It is at the moment.'

'But you can afford it,' said his father.

'Oh it's no trouble to me. And it'll become cheaper as more and more people take it up. Which they undoubtedly will. In ten years it'll be in every house in the city.'

'So you will be a sort of pioneer.'

'I suppose I will,' Roderick said happily.

'One of the privileges of wealth. I used to dream of wealth when I was your age. I never thought I would have a son who would achieve it.'

'I wouldn't say I've achieved it yet, Father. There is still plenty of money out there to be made.'

'That's the spirit!'

As if to underscore his promise Roderick took a cigar case from his jacket and offered them to his brother and father. 'All the way from Havana!' he said.

There was silence, punctuated by appreciative grunts, as they warmed and lighted the treasured objects.

'I'm wondering,' said Tom, 'do you think you were born with the knack of making money, or is it something you have been able to learn?'

'A combination of both, I think,' said Roderick, well disposed to expound on the subject. 'I've had a lot of learning to do, and there's no substitute for experience. But I've always felt I had a sort of instinct for it. The day I started I just wanted to get on with it, see whether I have what it takes. I've been fortunate enough to find out that I have. Do you know what the most important thing in this game is? Apart from sheer hard work, of course.'

Alexander Russell's eyes were agog as he waited for the answer. Sheer hard work would have been his guess, and he strongly disapproved of this being taken for granted. 'Persistence?' he ventured.

'A head for numbers,' suggested Elizabeth.

'Information,' said Roderick. 'Those who are first to the information have a head start on the way the market is going to go.

Why, just last month I had some information from a chap I know who's in with the bigwigs at Gleeson's. Got wind of a promising find near the South Australian border. I was able to snap up some stock for next to nothing. As soon as the information became public the price went through the roof. I sold out at five times what I'd paid. Wouldn't have made money like that in a whole season here.'

'It sounds rather unfair,' said Elizabeth.

'Nature of the game, Mother. Of course you're taking a risk every time you buy. I've lost my money on occasion too, you know.'

'No, I mean the idea of being able to buy in cheaply before anyone else knows about it. It seems unfair for those who don't have the information.'

'That's the advantage of being in the know, m'dear,' said Alexander Russell. 'That's the game.'

Elizabeth Russell looked dubious.

Her husband was moved to remind her that the game was not for everybody, that those who joined in required strong nerves. At this point he could not help taking a glance at his elder son, who was listening to the conversation in silence. 'Strong nerves,' he repeated, turning back to Roderick. 'Ain't that right, m'boy?'

'I'd go so far as to say he needs the gambler's instinct,' said Roderick.

Elizabeth looked at her husband. He was principally known in the area as a gambler. The highlight of every year was the horse racing he organised at Easter time.

'Perhaps,' Alexander Russell said, 'I should have done the same as you.'

'Perhaps you should have, Father.'

'Farming is a game for mugs, especially out here. But we love it, don't we, Tom?'

Tom nodded. 'Perhaps farming is a game for gamblers too,' he suggested. He had stayed on the farm because he was needed, and after Roderick left he was needed all the more. He knew it would have killed his mother for his father to be abandoned by both his sons. But he had noticed his father's eyes flicker in his direction when he mentioned that the game was not for everybody. He wondered how well he would have done if he had had the chance, if he had simply walked out and taken it like his brother had done.

The moon was bright enough to see by, so Roderick accompanied Tom part of the way back to his place after dinner. Both horses knew the way without being directed.

Tom had married and built his house since Roderick had been away. He had built it in a position the brothers had often discussed as being the best on the property. It was part way up a small hill with a view all the way to the ranges.

'I'll pay you a visit tomorrow,' said Roderick. 'I'll look forward to seeing what you've built here.'

'It's not much,' said Tom. 'It's very small. I'm sure you wouldn't think anything of it after what you're used to.'

'Oh, I'm not used to anything all that grand.'

'That wasn't the impression I received at the dinner table. I thought you were living in the lap of luxury these days.'

'I may have exaggerated a little. The old man rather egged me on.'

'He certainly seems impressed by your achievements.'

Roderick gave a grunt.

Tom sensed that this might be a moment to probe, to re-establish, perhaps, the level of candour they had always shared. 'Do you really have electric lighting in your house?'

'Oh yes. But it's not my house. I'm renting rooms there from a family I know.'

'What about the money you're making? What have you actually achieved?'

Roderick considered for a moment. It was true that he had made a lot of money on one or two occasions. He could mention sums that would be certain to impress a fellow from the bush for whom money was still a physical commodity that could be weighed out in coins and pound notes. But he had also lost sums like that. The important thing, he said to his brother, was that he now had skin in the game. He knew how to play, or at least he knew a lot more than he had known when he started, and knowledge was everything. He felt well placed to ride whatever booms were to come, and to lock in his profits along the way. 'One thing I am convinced of,' he said, '– it's the only way to make real money. You'll never make a genuine penny out here on the land.'

'But…'

'But you love it out here, I know, and money isn't everything. Yes, I'll grant you that. But even so, it makes one hell of a difference if you know how to make a little of it. It can make the difference between being up here, and here.' To illustrate the different levels of survival he held out a hand in front of his chest, then lowered it to his belly. 'Perhaps I can do something to help you.'

'What do you mean?'

'I could make some money for you. You give me fifty pounds and I'll guarantee to double it for you.'

Tom laughed. 'That would be impossible, I'm afraid.'

'All but guarantee, then.'

'I mean it would be impossible for me to give you fifty pounds. We simply don't see that sort of money out here.'

'But you have a bank account. There must be money in that.'

'There might be a few pounds floating about under the name of Drumwhindle. Hardly the sort of money that would interest you, I think.'

'Don't you have money of your own?'

'I've never had the need. If I have to buy something I go to the old man and he gives me the cash. He's perfectly generous.'

'So you can't spend a single penny without him knowing about it.'

'But it really doesn't matter. I hardly ever have to buy anything. He tells me when he buys things as well.'

'I'm sure he does. Even so, you should have your own wages. The farm is an income-producing entity. You should be paid a wage. You should be paid a wage for the work you do and you should keep it in your own bank account. Every man should have his own money.'

Tom said nothing. He understood the sense of what his brother was saying, but the truth was that the present arrangement suited him. He had never been comfortable with money unless it was a physical presence in his hand ready to be swapped for an immediate need. So far he had been able to organise his life without it.

'In the city, nobody would stand for working conditions like this.'

'It's different there. I feel part of Drumwhindle, and Drumwhindle is part of me.'

'I'm only offering to help, you know.'

'I understand that. But as you can see, it just wouldn't be possible.'

'Well, the offer will always be there.'

After this they changed the conversation completely. Both of them knew every inch of the property. They had been born here and had roamed it together as boys and helped their father fashion it into a viable living as soon as they were old enough. Tom had never left it. Every hill held a memory, every creek bed had the capacity to unleash a torrent of shared recollections. Soon they were happily splashing through them, losing themselves in the past. At last Tom started to glimpse the brother he had known, the lively half of him who had always wanted to take that next risk, on whom he had always been expected to act as a moderating influence but from whom, often, he had secretly taken the lead. It had been the loneliest day of his life when Roderick walked out. In fact it had given him the impetus he needed to go out and find himself a wife.

His house was visible now, perched part way up the hill in front of them, a dark cube in the moonlight. Inside it his wife and children would be sleeping. There were no lights in the windows but he knew she would have a couple of candles burning for him.

'Well,' said Roderick. 'I think this is where I should leave you.' Even in the light available he had been able to quickly size up the house that had been deemed suitable for his brother and his family, the maximum number of rooms a cube of that size could contain. He estimated it would fit into the homestead three times, possibly four. Tom had made desultory reference to taking over the homestead one day, but it sounded as though that day was far enough into the future to be ignored.

'I'll visit tomorrow. I'm looking forward to meeting Miriam and the children.'

It was a wonder to Tom that he had never met them. Suddenly it was brought to him how far apart they had travelled over the four years. He wanted to wake them all up and have the meeting now.

'I must say,' Roderick was saying, 'I feel a little envious of you right now, having them at home waiting for you.'

'It is something worth having,' said Tom. 'I've been very fortunate. What about your situation?'

'Oh, I have no "situation" to speak of. The ladies come, the ladies go. I'll make my choice when the time's right.'

'Make your choice?' Tom had gone out with a similar intention, but when he met Miriam there was no question of choice. There was just a terrible need that had to be satisfied. He would have liked to expand on the theme. Here was an area where he could possibly offer his brother some advice.

'I won't be dictated to,' Roderick said. 'I've got plenty of things to do before it's time to settle down. The ladies will come and go for a few years yet!'

'Maybe it won't work quite the way you're planning,' suggested Tom.

'Oh yes it will. I answer to nobody else. That was a promise I made to myself when I left this place. I've never seen any reason to break it.'

Tom abandoned the idea of advice.

They took their leave of each other. Roderick wheeled his horse around and returned down the well beaten track while Tom went on to his sleeping family.

Miriam, was still awake when Tom came in. He opened the door to the room where they slept and saw her lying on the bed with a candle burning on the dresser beside her. He took off his boots, came in and sat down on the edge of the bed, turning sideways to get past the cot where the boys were asleep.

'How was it?' she murmured.

'It was…all right. I've just said goodnight to him. He came with me almost as far as the house.'

'Did you recognise him after all this time? Is he the same brother you knew?'

Tom sighed and started to unpeel his stockings. 'No,' he said at last. 'He's not the same brother. He was little more than a boy when he left. He was hotheaded and a bit wild. Now, he's something else entirely. It's hard to know whether he's truly changed or whether he is putting on a face for his father.'

'I'm sure he would have changed after all this time. He would have grown up. And I expect he's nervous. It's been a long time.'

'Perhaps he is. But he seems the very opposite. He had father eating out of his hand.'

Miriam smiled. Anybody who could get the better of Alexander Russell had to be worth knowing.

'But there was something missing. At dinner it was all about how well he's doing, all the success he's having. In fact, I thought he was well on the way to becoming a pompous bore. It was only when we were riding back here that I had glimpses of the old Roderick. He admitted to me that he was not doing quite as well as he had presented it, and yet it's hard to understand how well he is doing. How much of what he's telling me is the truth?'

'Does it matter how well he is doing?'

'It matters whether he's telling the truth. It wasn't something I even thought of questioning before. I mean, if he lied it was about something obvious, usually with the intention of playing a trick on me.'

'Ssssh!' She put a finger to her lips and nodded towards the cot.

One of the boys was stirring. They watched in silence as the child stretched, whimpered and kicked out a foot. Then with a sigh he settled down again. Meanwhile, the other slept on, undisturbed.

They lay there for a while, listening to the silence on the plain, framed by the occasional cry of a lone plover.

Miriam had already heard enough to suggest a son who was turning into his father. It dismayed her to think there might be another Alexander Russell walking around after the first one was gone. She had married without even looking at the father but was now glad she had not done so, otherwise she might have missed out on Tom, who was nothing like his. He was gentle and considerate, always looking for the best in people. He would never make a fortune for them but he would never stop talking to her. She felt determined to do everything in her power to reconcile him with the brother he knew. 'When are we to meet him?' she whispered.

'He's to come over and see us tomorrow.'

'Good. We'll have a picnic.'

'I don't think he would be very used to picnics.'

'All the more reason to have one then. Everyone likes picnics, and it would be a perfect way for him to meet the boys.'

'All right then, a picnic it will be.' He knew she was right. She always was.

The next day, Miriam baked bread and a cake. The cake took three precious eggs. All morning the baking smell pervaded the house.

Outside, the boys rough and tumbled in anticipation. Their uncle Roderick was already popular with them. 'Unca Wodwick's coming!' they cried as they wrestled and somersaulted in the dust.

Tom watched them and wondered whether his brother would live up to expectations. He wondered whether Roderick would be good with the children. He rather thought he would be but there was always the possibility that he was wrong.

The dog joined the boys in the dust. She had come from one

of his father's litters and was supposed to be bred for cattle work. Alexander Russell had his own theories on the various levels of cruelty needed to mould a good dog. But this one had shown no aptitude for cattle work. She scattered them when she was supposed to round them up, allowed them to box her in and frighten her and barked excitedly when they were calm and settled. As a puppy she had been taken over by the boys and spoiled by their mother, and she quickly came to understand which side her bread was buttered. Alexander Russell equated the dog's deficiencies with certain deficiencies in his son's character, and a general lack of discipline around the home. Tom preferred to think of the dog as untrainable anyway and took comfort in the knowledge that his home fostered a certain degree of joy.

At noon Miriam took the bread and the cake out of the oven and set them on the kitchen table to cool. She took the previous day's lamb out of the cellar and cut two dozen slices onto a plate. She placed a second plate over the top of them and put it in a basket.

They had already decided on their picnic spot. It was their favourite one, on a hill across the valley where there were plenty of trees for shade and some rocks to provide a good clean surface. They would make a fire for the tea – that was something the boys always enjoyed. It was a bit of a walk but that was no bad thing as it would tire them out, and if they were unable to walk any further there would be two men to carry them.

At the main house, Elizabeth Russell showed her son the improvements she had been making to the garden. It had been almost bare when he had left but she had found solace and a source of supplies in the daily activity. There were several new beds, mostly given over to vegetables but in which she had also managed to keep alive something resembling a border. There was an arbour with two climbing roses for which she still had elaborate plans. There were various new shrubs and bushes and there was an area that she was turning, rock by back-breaking rock, into a sort of terrace.

The only thing that remained and that was familiar to him was the tangle of lantana in front of the porch which was growing more and more to resemble his father's mutton-chop whiskers. Nevertheless, compared with the upheavals he had been through, his mother's plans seemed stiflingly unambitious. He almost felt like walking away there and then, back to his other life, in case he was somehow dragged in. 'Do you mean to say,' he said, 'that you've done all this by yourself?'

'Tom helps me with the heavier rocks. But yes, apart from that I've managed it without a hand from anyone. You see, your old mother isn't as weak and feeble as you'd thought.'

'I never thought she was!' Roderick placed his arm across her shoulders and squeezed.

It was not quite a hug, but Elizabeth Russell felt for the first time a trace of the boy who used to throw his arms around her at the drop of a hat. She tried to sink in but he had already pulled away.

An hour later, Roderick was on his way into town with his father.

'I've got a treat for you,' said Alexander Russell.

'What is it?'

'I can't tell you that at the moment.' His father winked. 'You'll have to come with me and find out.'

'But I'd planned to go over to Tom's place. I was going to meet his boys. And his wife, of course.'

'They'll still be there when you get back. This will not wait.'

It was an hour into town in the spring cart. As they rode across the plain Roderick looked at the big wide sky and wondered what had kept him away for so long. Of course he knew that it was the man sitting beside him, or at least his perception of him. The arguments had come about almost daily towards the end. But now something had changed fundamentally between them. His father had not once tried to impose his will on him, unless you counted the current situation, but even with this he had been enabled to feel he was doing him a favour by acceding to his wish. Even more than that, he felt he now had something to offer his father.

Perhaps Alexander Russell's thoughts were running on similar lines, for he said, 'Do you remember the last time you rode across the plain?'

Roderick knew what he was referring to. It was the day he had left four years ago and he had not ridden, he had walked. Tom had accompanied him but his father had preferred to go in the other direction, insisting, as a way of emphasising Roderick's abandonment of them, upon some task that would not wait.

Alexander Russell looked across at his son. The pattern on his coat was still visible, the way his own had been when it was just bought. Now his, ingrained with several years' worth of dust, had taken on the colour of the land, whereas Roderick's proclaimed his detachment from it. It was the same with his boots. Although they were covered by their own coating of dust it was easy to see the polish quietly gleaming beneath it. 'I'm glad you're doing well,' he said. 'If I'd been asked that day, I would have predicted your return with your tail between your legs before the year was out. And I would have been pleased to see it. There's nothing a stubborn old fool likes so much as vindication. But now it looks as though the vindication was yours.'

'I don't think of myself as vindicated. I was hotheaded in those days, I'll admit to that. And it was pure hotheadedness that drove me away, just as it was stubbornness that kept me from coming back. There were many times when I wanted to but I wouldn't let myself, especially after the things that had been said.'

Alexander Russell remembered some of those things. They were not, on balance, things he would have chosen to repeat if he'd had the chance to say them again, but at the same time, he had not particularly regretted them because they had fulfilled a need at the time. Now he was prepared to draw some of their venom. 'No, I am glad you're doing well. I'm pleased to have a son with the spirit to go out and make something of himself.'

But presumably, thought Roderick, equally glad not to have two sons like that.

'It must be a very different world you live in,' said Alexander Russell.

'Very different.'

'Exciting too, I should imagine.'

'It is. Every day there's something new. People appear out of nowhere, burn like comets and disappear. Every day you see fortunes made and lost. There are opportunities everywhere you look, but there are dozens of men competing for every one.'

'I expect you have to keep your wits about you.'

'I do. Everybody does. And I will admit, in the beginning there were many times when I was caught out, when I didn't think quickly enough and lost out to someone else. But I didn't give up and every time I lost out I learned another thing not to do. Eventually I turned the corner and now I win more times than I lose.'

'You make it sound like a horse race.'

'In many ways it is. You make your choice and place your wager. The difference is that there are a lot more things you can do to stack the odds in your favour.'

'I've sometimes wondered,' said Alexander Russell, 'whether I wouldn't have been more suited to the money game.'

'I'm sure you would have succeeded if you had chosen that course.' Roderick looked across at his father, at the dust ingrained in his trousers, at the skin like leather on the backs of his hands. He was an influential man in the circles in which he moved. But those circles and the world he was describing were different in almost every way. He had known both. There was almost no point of contact between them. Those leathery hands were good for what they did.

At this point Alexander Russell seemed to lean a little closer to his son. The reins loosened in his hands and the horse continued of its own accord. 'I was wondering,' he said. 'I have some money put away... With your success... I was never averse, you know, to a little speculation.'

'I thought there was no money saved.'

'What made you think that?'

'Tom told me that. He said everything Drumwhindle makes is spent preparing for the following season.'

'Of course, he's quite correct. Technically this is not the farm's money. This is what I've put away on my own behalf. There's no reason for him to know about it. I've always fancied a little speculation, but there's so little opportunity for it out here. I thought in view of your success, and your superior information... Of course, I wouldn't expect you to do anything without some reward for yourself as well...'

Roderick nodded thoughtfully. He straightened his back. 'There's a small mining company out west,' he said, 'speculating in an area no one else has yet been. I've had some information...looking positive...opportunity to get in right at the beginning. If it does what I believe it's going to, there'll be huge rewards for both of us.'

'Splendid!' Alexander Russell all but slapped his son across the shoulders.

'I can't guarantee anything, of course.'

'Of course, I understand completely. But with your information…'

'I think we can say that the odds are in our favour.'

'Splendid! Absolutely splendid!'

The cake came out of the oven and was set down on the table to cool beside the bread. The smell attracted the children, the dog, even a chicken or two. Miriam shooed them all away without discrimination. The kitchen was hot and simply not large enough for any bodies other than her own.

'When Unca Wodwik coming?' shrieked the children as they skipped back into the bright outdoors.

'Soon,' Miriam assured them, 'and then we'll go on our picnic.'

The boys shrieked again and tumbled in the dust with the dog.

Miriam wondered whether it would be worth trying to wash their faces before her brother-in-law turned up. She decided against it. If she did so she would have to keep them away from the dust until he arrived for it to have any effect and she did not know how long that would be. Did she have any need to impress her brother-in-law? He would quickly see how they lived; the cottage with its three little rooms, the patched clothing, the paltry larder. If he had a mind to look down on them he would not have to search for reasons. Perhaps though, he would sense something else that was markedly absent from the main house at Drumwhindle; a lightness of atmosphere that had nothing to do with the finish of the timber on the walls or the range of supplies in the larder. Her mother-in-law had noticed it and remarked on it whenever she came to visit, which she had been doing more and more frequently. Once she had even seemed to hint that she would prefer to live here than the main house.

An hour later and the boys were hungry. Miriam cut the crust off each end of a loaf and gave it to them, smeared with jam and butter.

'Where Unca Wodwik?' came the cry again. For them he was rapidly approaching the status of a mythical figure, whose very arrival would release all the good things of the picnic.

'Maybe he's lost,' said Miriam. 'Maybe he's forgotten where we are.'

'He knows the property as well as I do,' said Tom. 'He would never get lost.'

'Perhaps he's forgotten, then. Why don't you ride over and see? I can't hold the boys back much longer. One way or another we'll have to have our picnic soon.'

Tom looked at the boys standing at the other side of the yard.

One of them had dropped his crust in the dirt and they were now examining what was left with expressions of the utmost seriousness.

'I don't think we should wait any longer,' Tom said. 'We'll leave him a note. He can join us when he turns up.'

The town in the middle of the afternoon was dusty and empty. None of its dozen or so stores was open, although some labourers could be spied enjoying an illicit grog behind the closed doors of their favourite watering hole.

Alexander Russell guided the cart up the main street and turned into an alleyway where he found some shade to hitch the horse.

'The mystery deepens,' said Roderick. 'Where on earth are you taking me, Father?'

Alexander Russell smiled to himself. 'We may be lacking in a lot of the city's pleasures out here, but not all of them.' He took a key out of the pocket of his jacket and tossed it like a coin. He led his son to a large house that stood by itself in another dusty yard.

There was a deep veranda along the side facing them but, although there were several chairs, no one was taking advantage of its shade. Ignoring the front door, Alexander Russell went to the dark end of the veranda and unlocked a much smaller one.

Inside, Roderick was surprised to find a veneer of opulence that had not been suggested by the exterior. Sunlight was excluded by thick curtains, walls were draped with silk and there were armchairs and sofas on the carpeted floor. In the corner, three men played cards by the light of a kerosene lamp. Two of them were smoking clay pipes and their faces were partly obscured by the resulting haze. Normally, he would have taken the chance and offered a greeting, but that sort of behaviour seemed to be constrained here.

'Come.' Alexander Russell ushered his son through into the next room.

It was divided from the first by a pair of thin wooden doors. From a cupboard he took a bottle of whisky and poured a drink for each of them. This room, like the first, was heavily curtained but there was another small window above the curtains which let in enough of the bright afternoon to see by.

Roderick sipped at the raw whisky. It had never been his drink but in this place he felt almost obliged to follow his father's lead. The spirit burned his tongue but it provided some other employment for it than talking.

Presently, they heard voices approaching them from one of the rooms still further inside.

A woman's was saying, 'I told you. Didn't I tell you?'

Another voice, higher in pitch but quite uncowed, replied, 'No you didn't.'

The owner of the first voice entered the room where the men were sitting. She was a large woman with a red face and visible beads of sweat below her hairline. She grinned when she saw them.

Roderick noticed that his father did not rise to his feet when he greeted her.

'Haven't seen you for a while,' the woman said in a mildly reproachful tone.

'It's only been a few weeks,' Alexander Russell insisted. He turned to Roderick. 'They don't let you get away with anything,' he said in a tone that indicated he was not entirely displeased with the situation. He introduced his son.

The woman raised an eyebrow and remarked that she was sure he would not regret his visit.

Roderick, sufficiently attuned to the nuance of the place not to rise to his feet for the introduction, expressed the hope that she would be proved correct.

She went back into the room from which she had emerged.

Through the half-open door Roderick caught a glimpse of a bare brown breast and he knew that his hope would be fulfilled.

Tom blew gently on the embers and added more dried grass. A twist of smoke appeared, the flame beneath it all but invisible in the sunlight. The boys stood ready, each with a handful of sticks. When their father gave the word, they opened out their hands and released their little bundles with the peculiar, impulsive motion that is the preserve of the very young. Tom picked up the fallen sticks and laid them where they would be best positioned to catch the young flame.

There had been no more talk of Uncle Roderick. He had been

wiped from their minds once they understood he was not coming after all, replaced by an early block in the wall of mistrust with which a young mind gradually learns to perceive. Instead they had their grandmother, less exciting but more dependable, who had turned up in his place.

She could be relied upon to take an interest in the things they found as they rushed around the picnic site. She was sitting up there on the flat rock, deep in conversation with their mother. She had turned up just as they were about to set off, with the news that Roderick and his father had gone to town and would not be back until the evening.

'But we'd arranged for Roderick to come over here,' said Tom.

'He asked me to give you his apologies,' Elizabeth lied.

'What's so urgent in town that he has to break his appointment?' asked Miriam.

'I have no idea. I can only imagine that Alexander already had the errand in mind and that Roderick did not want to disappoint his father.'

'So he's disappointed us instead,' said Miriam.

'I'm sure there'll be other opportunities,' said Tom. 'I wouldn't put it quite so strongly as to say we had made an appointment. It was something less formal than that. Perhaps he'll come and see us tomorrow.'

'Who knows? We don't even know how long he's planning to stay. He might be intending to leave tomorrow.' Miriam attempted to sound bitter but in reality the identity of her brother-in-law was fast merging in her mind with that of her father-in-law and she was not now unhappy that he had decided to stay away.

Elizabeth was invited to join the picnic in Roderick's place, an offer she accepted without reluctance.

The spring cart made its way back through the empty Sunday streets.

It was not until they were back out on the plain that Alexander Russell broke the silence. 'Well?' he said to his son. 'How was it?'

'It was fine,' said Roderick. 'It was just fine.'

'I particularly asked for you to have little Rose. She's new and fairly fresh but she knows a trick or two.'

At this point the cart lurched. The horse, its head inside a cloud of flies, had given it a good shake, become unsighted and dragged a hoof across a banked up wheel rut.

'Caarn!' Alexander Russell shook the reins.

The cart lurched the other way and the horse regained its stride. The two men were thrown against each other but quickly regained their places.

'So,' Alexander Russell persisted, 'what did you think of her?'

'She was very nice.'

'Knows a trick or two, doesn't she?'

'Yes.'

'Next time I think I'll take her. You might like her sister.'

Roderick watched the sun against the hills in the distance. At this time of day they always started to turn a delicate pink. He had hardly even been aware of little Rose and her tricks. The thought of his rutting father in the room next door had severely dampened his enthusiasm. Now he felt cheated, soiled and alone.

'We may not have all the pleasures of the big smoke but we still have our fun.'

'You do,' said Roderick. 'You do.'

The two women perched on the sun-warmed rock, while the children rushed about in the shade below and their father set about his tea-making ministrations in unhurried silence. Miriam removed her boots and her stockings and stretched out her bare legs.

Tom had his braces hanging by his sides. Squatting there by the fire he looked like a huge bird.

She laughed at the sight of him. He was asking to be teased. 'Tom!' she called. 'Hurry up, would you. We're dying of thirst up here!'

Tom looked around and grinned.

'I'll have mine with milk and sugar. Just the right amounts, mind. You'll not get away with anything that is less than perfect!'

'Madam shall have what Madam desires.' He executed a salute and an obsequious little bow that had both women rocking with laughter.

The boys returned from their scavenging with handfuls of sun-bleached bones. They held them up for their father's inspection.

'You're a chook!' the younger one suddenly said.

Tom made wings with his elbows and chased them around the fire, making ponderous clucking sounds. The boys squealed with laughter as they tried to stay ahead of him. The sounds of all their laughter filled the picnic site.

Born and educated in England, Angus Gaunt has been in Australia since 1987. He now lives with his family in Sydney. These stories were all written on the 7.22 between Normanhurst and Central.